ANNABELLE'S BIG MOVE

Carla Golembe

Story One: Annabelle's New Home

Story Two: Annabelle's New Friends

Houghton Mifflin Company
Boston

ANNABELLE'S

NEW HOME

It snowed almost every day where Annabelle lived.

After playing outside she liked to sleep on her blanket by the fireplace.

Sometimes in her dreams she could smell summer.

One day Annabelle's family put all of their things into boxes.

Strong men came to their house.

"Stop!" barked Annabelle.

She didn't know where they were going.

"Come back!" Annabelle barked, but her family just waved good-bye.

"Where am I?" she wondered.

After a long time . . .

Annabelle saw her family. "Good!" she thought.

"Now we can go home."

But when they started driving,
the world looked very different to Annabelle.

"There's a pretty house," she thought. "Who lives there?"

And do you know what her family said then?

"Welcome home, Annabelle!" they said.

Now Annabelle loves her new home.

And she likes to sleep by the open window, where it smells like summer — every night. Good night, Annabelle!

ANNABELLE'S

NEW FRIENDS

Annabelle loved her new house with the garden that bloomed all year round.

But she was lonely.

One day Miranda took her for a long walk.

She saw dogs who looked strange to her,
not like the dogs in her old neighborhood.

She did not say hello.

At the park Annabelle saw other dogs playing ball.

She wasn't sure if they would let her play. She did not say hello.

Then Miranda took Annabelle to a beach full of dogs.

"Go on, Annabelle," said Miranda. "Play with them."

The sea looked sparkly and fun. Annabelle wanted to play.

"Hello," she barked, but her bark was so quiet the other dogs
didn't hear. "HELLO!" Annabelle barked more loudly.

Then, from the edge of the sea, a spotted dog barked
back to Annabelle. Slowly, she stepped into the water.
It felt cold but exciting. Annabelle went in a little deeper.

A wave came and lifted her up.

Suddenly, her paws began to move in the fizzy rolling waves.

She was swimming!

Now Annabelle swims at Dog Beach every day with her new friends.

And when she gets home she takes a nice long nap.

Sweet dreams, Annabelle.

To Laurie Kaplowitz and Donna Calleja —
old friends through many moves

In celebration of Annabelle

LIBRARY OF CONGRESS CATALOGING-IN-PUBLICATION DATA

Golembe, Carla.
Annabelle's big move / written and illustrated by Carla Golembe.
p.   cm.
Summary: In two stories, a dog must adjust when her family moves
to a new house and she makes new friends on a visit to the beach.
ISBN 0-395-91543-0
[1. Dogs—Fiction.]   I. Title.
PZ7.G5814An   1999
[E]—dc21   98-10970   CIP   AC

Printed in Singapore
TWP 10 9 8 7 6 5 4 3